P9-DEG-649

For two gifts from heaven,
Maéva and Anaïs

— G. T.

For Charles and Antoine

— B. St-A.

Nicholas was happily reading in bed when his dad barged into the room.

"Guess what, son? The goalie on your team is sick. How do you feel about playing in net tomorrow?"

"Sure!" said Nicholas, without thinking. "No problem!"

The Best Goalie Ever

by
Gilles Tibo

illustrations by
Bruno St-Aubin

Scholastic Canada Ltd.
New York Toronto London Auckland Sydney
Mexico City New Delhi Hong Kong Buenos Aires

Scholastic Canada Ltd.
604 King Street West, Toronto, Ontario M5V 1E1, Canada

Scholastic Inc.
557 Broadway, New York, NY 10012, USA

Scholastic Australia Pty Limited
PO Box 579, Gosford, NSW 2250, Australia

Scholastic New Zealand Limited
Private Bag 94407, Botany, Manukau 2163, New Zealand

Scholastic Children's Books
Euston House, 24 Eversholt Street, London NW1 1DB, UK

Library and Archives Canada Cataloguing in Publication
Tibo, Gilles, 1951-

The best goalie ever / Gilles Tibo ; illustrations by Bruno St-Aubin ; translation by Petra Johannson.
Translation of: Nicolas, roi du filet!. For ages 4-7.
ISBN 978-0-545-98072-2

I. St-Aubin, Bruno II. Johannson, Petra III. Title. IV. Title: Nicolas, roi du filet! English.

PS8589.I26N4313 2009   jC843'.54   C2009-901735-0

ISBN-10 0-545-98072-0

Text copyright © 2009 by Gilles Tibo.
Illustrations copyright © 2009 by Bruno St-Aubin.
Translation by Petra Johannson.
English text copyright © 2009 by Scholastic Canada Ltd.
All rights reserved.

No part of this publication may be reproduced or stored in a retrieval system, or transmitted in any form or
by any means, electronic, mechanical, recording, or otherwise, without written permission of the publisher,
Scholastic Canada Ltd., 604 King Street West, Toronto, Ontario M5V 1E1, Canada. In the case of photocopying
or other reprographic copying, a licence must be obtained from Access Copyright (Canadian Copyright Licensing
Agency), 1 Yonge Street, Suite 800, Toronto, Ontario M5E 1E5 (1-800-893-5777).

6 5 4 3 2 1   Printed in Canada   09 10 11 12 13

Mixed Sources
Product group from well-managed
forests and other controlled sources
www.fsc.org Cert no. SGS-COC-003098
© 1996 Forest Stewardship Council
FSC

His dad tucked him in and kissed him goodnight.
Nicholas lay in the dark, his eyes wide open.
He kept thinking, *I… I… I've never stopped a puck
in my life!*

Nicholas just couldn't get to sleep. To get his mind off the game, he looked out the window. The moon was like a giant hockey puck. The clouds were like huge nets. The stars were champion shooters — and they were about to score on his net! Nicholas was worried. He lay awake, wishing tomorrow would never come.

Seconds, minutes and hours ticked by.
Nicholas couldn't sleep a wink. When
morning came, he was completely exhausted.

His dad rushed in. "Hurry, Nicholas! The coach dropped off the equipment. The team is waiting for you at the rink!"

Nicholas got out of bed. His eyes were barely open. He skidded on a racing car. BAM! He crashed to the floor.

Half asleep, he headed for the kitchen.
WHAM! He walked into the door frame.

He sat down at the table. SPLOOSH!
Face-first into the cereal bowl.

He tried to brush his teeth. ZZZZZ…
He fell asleep against the mirror.

While Nicholas dozed, his family tried to get him into the goalie gear. It wasn't easy because he was so floppy. All he was dreaming about was sleep, sleep and more sleep!

At last Nicholas was all geared up. He managed to stuff himself into the car, goalie pads and all.

His dad looked at his watch. "We're going to be late!" he said.

He stepped on the gas. VROOM!
Nicholas snoozed, dreaming that he
was back in bed.

SCREECH! The car came to a halt
outside the arena. Nicholas bolted awake.
His dad checked his watch again.
"Come on, Nicholas! The game starts
in three minutes!"

They hurried through the doors into the arena. Nicholas's heart stopped. The stands were packed. His team was warming up on the ice. The coach rushed over. "Okay, Nicholas! Go get in net!"

His dad gave him a wink and a tap on the helmet. "Go on, Nicholas! You're the best!"

Nicholas headed for the net. His heart was pounding. He took a look at the opposing players. They seemed huge — and mean. It was like a bad dream.

The game began. Nicholas could barely keep his eyes open. All through the first period, he yawned and stretched — and stopped the puck. The crowd cheered.

He dropped to his knees to rest a little
— and made more saves. The crowd
cheered and bounced in their seats.

In the second period, Nicholas was even sleepier. He leaned on one goalpost, then the other — and stopped more pucks. The crowd cheered, bounced in their seats and threw their arms in the air!

In the third period, Nicholas was so drowsy that he dropped to the ice for a nap. He stopped even *more* pucks! The crowd cheered, bounced in their seats and threw their arms in the air, chanting NI-CHO-LAS! NI-CHO-LAS! NI-CHO-LAS! while they did the wave.

At last the game was over. Nicholas's team had won 6–0! There was a standing ovation. Nicholas's teammates rushed over to congratulate him and carry him on their shoulders. But he was too groggy to smile.

In the change room, the coach told Nicholas's dad, "Your son is amazing. He's a natural goalie. He anticipates the shots! He's so laid-back! What cool! What leadership!"

"Um, yes, he amazed us all," said his dad proudly.

But Nicholas didn't hear any more.
He was fast asleep — at last!